Mult

David Winship

Copyright © 2020 David Winship

All rights reserved.

ISBN: 9781674744575

Dedicated to everyone who suspects that one of the poems is about them.......
Yes, one of them *is* about you and you'll have to buy the book to find it!

Acknowledgements

This book would not have been possible without the input of two people in particular: my wife, Bianca, for her ongoing support, and my friend, Judy, whose encouragement and editorial help have been invaluable to me.

iv

WARNING!
May contain traces of serious writing.

Two Wolves

This poem is based on a legend believed to have been passed down from generation to generation of the Cherokee Native American tribe.

Two wolves are always fighting
In each and every soul.
How can we know for certain
Which one will take control?

One wolf is proud and hostile
And snarls with every lope.
The other wolf has empathy
And eyes alight with hope.

I asked my dad which wolf will win.
His words were wise indeed.
He thought a while, then told me:
"Depends which one you feed."

No Protons, No Electrons and Just a Dash of Milk

The hydrogen atoms in water were formed right after the Big Bang nearly 14 billion years ago. They've been through all kinds of experiences. They could have come from stars (ancient supernovae explosions) and may have travelled to Earth on a comet. They may have then become part of the Earth's crust, only to be spat out again by a volcano. At some point they may have been part of other living organisms……. before they temporarily become part of our bodies when we drink a cup of tea!

Please tell the manager I'm quite displeased!
I really don't mean to be rude,
But, according to this science article here,
Our tea is not freshly brewed!

It says here some atoms in our tea
Are as old as time itself!
I assumed your stuff was impeccably fresh
And perfectly good for our health.

These atoms were born at the dawn of time -
And they may have come from the stars!
So should they be sipped and slurped and gulped
In tea shops and coffee bars?

I don't want to make an unseemly fuss -
Your cups are commendably clean -
But we can't have hydrogen in our tea...
We just don't know where it's been!

Those Two Impostors

Lines from Rudyard Kipling's poem 'If' are inscribed above the entrance to Wimbledon's Centre Court. They exhort us to treat triumph and disaster as equals.

I'm sure Rudyard Kipling was a lovely chap,
But how could he write such confusing crap?
If triumph and disaster are just the same,
Then why do we bother to play this game?
If Kipling was here, I'd give him the news…
It feels a LOT better to win than lose!

I never overthink things. It's not that I'm not smart enough to do it. It's just that *under*thinking is my new ninja thing.

Sorry!

Some people apologise excessively and compulsively. It may be a behavioural trait that stems from anxiety or low self-esteem. Clinical psychologists might say it's indicative of a hyperactive amygdala. Whatever. Apologies aren't always helpful or sincere. On the other hand, people with narcissistic personality disorder rarely, if ever, apologise. For relationships to function normally, a balance has to be found whereby both parties recognise their role in a conflict. I'm sorry I brought this subject up. I feel terrible now.

I apologise for ev'rything,
Even when I'm not to blame!
I apologise for Donald Trump,
And I'm sorry for the rain.

I'm responsible for the roadworks
When your car comes to a halt.
When a penguin learns that it can't fly,
It's clearly all my fault.

Should you decide that reading this stuff
Was not worth the time that it took,
I guess the buck must stop with me -
I'm sorry I wrote the book!

A Trip to Mars

The challenge of space exploration
Is one we should take up anew.
The last time humans set foot on the moon
Was 1972.

Our planet's incredibly fragile -
We don't know how long it'll last.
An asteroid might be heading this way -
It's happened here in the past.

Dinosaurs made no contingency plans
For asteroids coming along.
The lack of a valid space programme
Is where I think they went wrong!

They say they'd send people to Mars and back,
If it wasn't for the price.
Perhaps I should tell them I'd go for free,
If they asked me really nice?

Ikea

Ah yes, Ikea and that wonderful flat pack furniture... You spend a disproportionate amount of time looking for the right screw. When you find it, you spend ages screwing together one particular piece, only to find you've put it on backwards. The experience can seriously jeopardise your relationship with the person you're assembling the furniture with... And, then, finally, when you think you've got it all done, you realise there's either one piece missing or some really significant-looking pieces left over!

I thought it would be an awesome idea
To write a poem about Ikea.
So I assembled some words and made them rhyme,
Put them together in pretty good time.
I felt really chuffed and sat on the sofa,
And that's when I noticed the words left over!!

People tell me I wouldn't say 'boo' to a goose. But then, why *would* I? I bet those people haven't even tried it. A goose can give you quite a nip on the back of the leg.

When the Bubble Bursts

I think of the things we used to do
And the laughs we used to share.
How can it count for nothing at all?
Somehow it doesn't seem fair.

These things now strike a chord in my heart
And bring a tear to my eye.
I don't want to put them behind me
And I don't want to say goodbye.

We soared like a stock market bubble
Before it blew up and crashed.
Can our friendship ever recover?
Its value is all but trashed.

Investing in friendship's not easy:
A house of mirrors and smoke.
I'm s'posed to feel richer and wiser,
But something inside me is broke.

In a democracy, shouldn't there be room for those who don't want a fair society?

Six Minutes

Human civilisation is very young on the scale of cosmic time. To illustrate just how young it is, it might help to conceptualise the entire history of the universe within one calendar year...

It's hard for our poor brains to fathom
The sheer age of the universe.
You can read loads of stuff about it,
But you risk just making it worse!

Think of the timescale another way:
Let's try to grasp the idea
Of the history of the universe
Expressed as a calendar year.

New Year's Day arrives with a Big Bang,
And galaxies appear in the Spring.
By September our own solar system
Is formed on the Milky Way's wing.

When October arrives, it brings us
The first single cellular life.
By the time we're thinking of Christmas,
Dinosaurs and turtles are rife.

After Christmas, the branches erupt
On the evolutionary tree.
With just six minutes remaining,
The first human life comes to be.

Our story consigned to six minutes!
On that kind of scale, we're so small.
Although we think we're important,
Six minutes is nothing at all!

Birds on a Telegraph Wire

Two birds were perched on a telegraph wire,
Which is stranger than it might appear,
For one was a penguin from Antarctica,
The other a Peruvian rhea.

Anyway, there's nothing much else to tell – after a while I guess they just went their separate ways.

The Teapot

All the matter relating to a cosmic object like a star or a planet is pulled inward by the force of gravity, resulting in its spherical shape. Gravity also acts on a china teapot, but the teapot is far less massive than a star or a planet, so the effects are significantly weaker. Gravity is, in fact, no match for the other three fundamental forces of nature (the weak nuclear force, the strong nuclear force and electromagnetism). Even smaller cosmic objects like asteroids are not massive enough for gravity to overcome electromagnetism, so they retain their non-spherical shape. Although gravity cannot collapse the teapot itself into a sphere, it will try to make it part of a bigger sphere, i.e. the Earth. Consider what happens when you drop the teapot. Gravity ensures it falls to the ground, whereupon the electromagnetic bonds holding its atoms and molecules together are broken, compromising its integrity as an object. It shatters into pieces.

I hold a china teapot and contemplate its shape;
I wonder if its molecules consider an escape.
Gravity is weak, they say - the weakest force for sure.
I think I'll lend a helping hand..........
                                and
                                drop
                                it
                                on
                                the
                                floor!

Friends

Obviously, not all friendships are worth saving and devotion to one can sometimes be unhealthy, especially if there's an imbalance of giving and taking. When you're faced with the possible breakup of a friendship, the dynamic is so complex and... well, how do you ever really know what's best? Anyway, here's some advice my late mother gave me.

If you're blessed with friends that really care,
Make sure you keep them close.
Don't let them fade into thin air
Like transitory ghosts!

If they always check that you're okay
And hold you when you weep,
If they listen to the things you say,
They're friends that you should keep.

They're fragile, rare and elusive.
Love them and hold them dear!
If they sense you no longer need them,
They might just disappear.

Dark Matter

Dark matter is a mysterious invisible substance thought to be responsible for much of the mass in the universe. It's not made of the same stuff as the matter we're familiar with. We just assume it exists because its gravitational effects are the only explanation for certain cosmic phenomena. Astronomers, for example, have observed galaxy clusters crashing into each other at high speed. They expected a scattering of the stars, gas and dust, but when they studied the aftermath of the collision, they discovered a gravitational pull generated by what appeared to be an empty area of space.

Could something similar prevail in the human psyche?

When blue devils arrive and threaten
To obliterate my heart,
A weird hypothetical substance
Prevents it from falling apart.

Without it, feelings would fly unchecked
Into a cosmic psychic mist.
We cannot directly observe it,
But we know that it must exist.

When my heart spins off into deep space,
This strange gravitational force
Invisibly holds it together
And sets it back on its course.

Laryngitis

I've lost my voice completely now -
I must have worn it out!
No one listens to me anyway…
Not even when I

S
H
O
U
T
!

Insert Name Here

That awkward moment when someone greets you like a long-lost friend and you can't remember who on earth they are...

I have to admit I feel glum -
Forgetting her name was just dumb!
I could have just asked,
But the moment has passed;
I just know her as Beverley's mum!

I suppose I could have just guessed -
Maybe Emma or Hannah or Bess?
It would've been wrong
And I didn't have long,
And the right thing to do was confess.

But next time my brain will be clear,
I'll approach her without any fear.
Without feeling shy,
I'll greet her with 'Hi…
Can you please just insert your name here!'

The Universe in a Tennis Ball

For a split second after the Big Bang,
The universe was incredibly small…
Billions of galaxies were nothing more
Than the size of a tennis ball!

The next time we go to the tennis club,
Here's a thing we don't normally do…
Let's open a new tube of tennis balls
And pause for a moment or two.

We'll each take a tennis ball in our hands
And ponder this miracle together.
Or forget all this cosmology stuff…
And whack them with rackets? Whatever.

This book could easily be a million-seller.... if I could just get 999,999 more people to buy it!

The Faithful Moth

I never really questioned
All the faith I had in you.
I was heedless of your power,
Like a wave drawn to the moon.

I've often kind of wondered
What it's like to be a moth...
I think I now know how it feels
When the lamp has been switched off.

Forsaking the Poppy

It may seem natural to feel an allegiance with those who happen to occupy the same bit of the earth's crust as you do, but that allegiance is purely arbitrary and, of course, narrow and divisive. This is obviously controversial, but, as Samuel Johnson opined, isn't patriotism "the last refuge of a scoundrel"? Isn't it often synonymous with racism and chauvinism? Isn't it also, in some respects, the opiate of the masses?

Perhaps the time has come for us to envision a new era of humanity, moving from competing nation states to the flourishing of a multi-cultural planetary civilisation defined by universal kinship.

As Remembrance Day approaches,
Do you think it's impolite
To decline to wear a poppy?
Is it wrong or is it right?

Having died in the line of duty,
Where poppies now abound,
Those men of Flanders fields deserve
To hear the bugles sound.

But perhaps it's time to draw a line
And recognise at last
That saluting violent conflicts
Just roots us in the past.

Will soldiers have died for nothing
And will warfare ever cease,
If we hold a minute's silence
And our thoughts don't turn to peace?

Plucking the poppies from our coats
Is not really breaking faith;
It might just serve to help us
To create a world that's safe.

I've Changed My Mind

I change my opinions all the time,
I'm like a traffic light.
The strangest thing about it is...
I'm *still* always right!

Six Degrees of Separation

Six Degrees of Separation is a theory that contends that we're all connected through acquaintances to everyone else in the world by just six connections, i.e. you are one degree away from everyone you know, two degrees away from everyone they know, and so on.

Just six degrees of separation
Lie between us all.
In this age of social media,
The world is now so small.

But I've just disproved the theory!
I'm a hermit now, I think!
My connections are all broken -
My Wi-Fi's on the blink!

There is no wall so high and no river so wide that you can't just go home and eat pizza!

Paradoxically Pooped

When I read an email from a friend that was sent at 1.30 a.m., saying she was too tired to sleep, I thought that didn't make any sense, but...did it? A paradox is a statement that seems to contradict itself and defy common sense, but it may contain an underlying truth.

Sorry, but I can't guarantee any underlying truths here...

One baking hot December day
Or it may have been in June,
I think it was in the morning
Or maybe the afternoon,
I got a message from a friend
Who was much too tired to sleep!
Was this just frivolous nonsense?
Was I missing something deep?

They say it's called a paradox
To be too hungry to eat.
Well, although it seems confusing,
In a way it's kinda neat.

I've made you read this awful verse
And I pray that you don't mind.
It must be vaguely obvious
I'm being cruel to be kind.

Fear ye not, you are approaching
The beginning of the end.
The rule here is: ignore all rules -
That's what I recommend.

Perhaps my brain is worn out now
Or maybe it's on the blink.
The explanation I prefer
Is... I'm much too smart to think!

Tartan Trainers

Chloe was contagious.
She had the Scottish flu.
Her skin had turned to tartan,
Her brand-new trainers too!

"Noo jist haud on!" the doctor said.
"It's gaein be awright!
Jus' soak your skin in porridge
All day and overnight."

She duly smeared her face and hands,
Her brand-new trainers too!
By midnight she was fully cured
And felt like someone new!

She rushed out for a training run,
She had no time for sleep.
Her trainers burped and fell apart
And left her in a heap!

So listen to your doctor,
For that's the golden rule.
But though this works for people,
For shoes it's not so cool.

Cozzzmology

Just study science every day!
That's what my teacher used to say.
Apply your brain, you really must,
And blow away that mental dust!

I'm always glued to science books,
Ignoring those derisive looks
From friends who think I'm half insane
And tell me 'Dave, you should refrain!'

Well, tell me what could be more fun
Than learning all about the sun?
And when I think I've learned enough,
There's gluons, quarks and all that stuff.

'Cos leptons rock, you can't deny!
And quarks and bosuns, both, oh my!
And every time a few collide,
A new one gets identified!

But people don't seem too impressed,
They look so bored I must confess,
I talk to friends, they start to snore!
I don't know why that is, I'm sure.

So sub-atomic particles
Have made me turn out farcical,
For now each time I start to speak…
Well, even *I* just fall asleep!

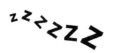

Make It Snow This Christmas

This is the lyric for a song my daughter, Lisa, and I wrote when she was a teenager. It's written from the perspective of a mother who has recently separated from her husband. Christmas is approaching and she's talking to her child.

I know what you want on Christmas Day,
I know what it is you're wishing,
But you know he's had to go away.
I'm sorry, but he'll be missing.

I'll do anything I can for you,
I know all your hopes and wishes,
But I cannot make your dreams come true,
I can't make it snow this Christmas.

Christmas could be such a perfect day,
With bells, mistletoe and holly,
But when he's gone so far away,
It's hard to be happy and jolly.

He loves you still and so do I;
It's not your fault we've parted.
Christmas is not a time to cry…
And now you've got me started.

I'll do anything I can for you,
I know all your hopes and wishes.
If I could make one dream come true,
I'd make it snow this Christmas.

'Owellojello' Gemma

I knew someone once who embellished a lot of the words and phrases she used with a rhyme. So 'awesome' became 'awesome-saucesome' and 'oh well' became 'owellojello'...

'Owellojello' Gemma
Presented a dilemma.
We were so confused
By the lingo she used,
But who would dare to tell her?

We lived in her neighbourhood,
So we did the best we could -
There *were* a few times
We deciphered her rhymes,
But we still called her Miss Understood.

All of us can remember
That day back in November,
When she first came to fame
And we all spoke the same
As 'Owellojello' Gemma!

Imagine if people were born with a remote........ you could press the channel button and get them to change the subject, you could shut them up by pressing mute (or use the volume control button) and you could get subtitles when they're not making any sense. On my TV remote, there's a button labelled SMART – wow, I know certain people who would love to try switching me into *that* mode!.... No, no, no, please don't press my standby button!

Silenced by the Bullet

When I think of peaceful protest,
A man in khadi comes to mind.
An eye for an eye, he told us,
Would only make us blind.

I think of a march for freedom,
The man who had a dream:
His visions from a mountaintop,
The promised land he'd seen.

When Vietnam burned, another man
Protested from his bed:
"Imagine there's no country!
Give peace a chance!" he said.

Great icons of our history,
Such men of great renown…
Why did they meet hostility?
Why did they get shot down?

Dominique

She pursed her lips as she placed her chips,
But her chances were very bleak.
The man with the rake gave his head a shake
At poor old Dominique.

And all of her friends fretted and frowned,
Though none of them dared to speak.
"In for a penny, in for a pound!"
Said daring Dominique.

She thought she'd win with one last fling
And banish her losing streak.
"Fortune sides with those who dare!"
Said deluded Dominique.

She asked me to call out a number
From zero to thirty-six.
I said: "Be brave and bet on yer age!"
And we sat there quite transfixed.

No one was sure why she fell to the floor.
"What 'appened?" said I to the dealer.
"She put all 'er chips on twenty-six,

Then I could no longer see 'er."

We all had a beer and it soon became clear
Why she'd turned so pale and weak,
For the wheel had stopped at thirty-three:
The *true* age of Dominique!

Pieces of Truth

They don't know when it happened.
Was it way back in the past?
Was it one almighty crash?
Was it slow or was it fast?

The TV crews all missed it,
The politicians too,
The drunkards in the downtown bar
Just didn't have a clue.

A lawyer found some on the street
And stopped to take a look.
He sold some to a victim
And he sold some to a crook.

A priest came by and took a piece
And kept it to himself.
He soon had a collection,
All dusty on his shelf.

A million little pieces
Scattered all around.
No one saw it coming
It never made a sound.
No one really noticed…
The day that Truth fell down.

Checkmate

I was challenged to a game of chess
By a friend who came to stay.
I had an hour or two to spare,
So I agreed to play.

I admit I took a lot of time
Over my initial move.
I think I looked inscrutable -
Chess masters would approve.

But after half an hour he left -
Perhaps I'd psyched him out?
Chess is such a mental game,
Of that there is no doubt.

Perhaps he went to contemplate
The plan of my attack.
The truth is I just wasn't sure
If I was white or black!

Please will you explain to me
The peculiar words he used.
Those molecules and wavelengths
Have got me all confused.

Really? Weren't you listening
To a single word he said?
The sky appears to us so blue...
Because it isn't red!

Random

I like pushing my luck around
And pulling people's legs.
It's how I get my exercise
While scoffing ham and eggs.

It rained so much these last few days,
It never seemed to stop.
The sky's completely empty now
It's squeezed out ev'ry drop!

What on earth connects this stuff?
I haven't got a clue!
That's why I *so* like poetry –
I just leave it up to you!

Lunch Breaks

Isn't a happy workforce likely to be more productive?

We're officially at crisis point,
The town hall folks are stumped,
The economy is on its knees
And retail sales have slumped.

What could have caused this trouble?
Where does the problem lurk?
And why are fingers pointing at
The office where I work?

Half-eaten rolls and sandwiches
Are flowing out the door -
An avalanche of snacks and drinks
Like no one's seen before.

I'll now reveal it's all because
We don't have time to munch.
The manager has given us
Just half an hour for lunch!

Over the Edge

A lunar eclipse (flat-earth style)!

Fifty years after one of mankind's greatest achievements, there's a disturbing number of moon landing deniers. They're joined by flat-earthers, climate change deniers, anti-vaccination quacks and others, all of whom contribute to a growing trend of anti-scientific thinking and stand in the way of progress and societal development.

A friend of mine is quite convinced
That Earth is really flat.
I bite my tongue for I would hate
To get into a spat.
I show him a photograph
Of Earth taken from space -
But he believes Apollo missions
Never did take place.

Earth's shadow, I say, is clearly curved
During a full eclipse.
He tells me that proves nothing,
So I just purse my lips,
And as we take a long, long walk,
I make a solemn pledge:
I'll make sure he keeps walking till…
He falls over the edge.

After insisting that his flat-earth belief was scientifically unviable… I then made the mistake of telling him the universe is flat!! ☺

The End of the Universe or the Big Munch

Assuming the universe contains sufficient dark energy, then it will theoretically continue forever. If, however, that is not the case, gravity will put the brakes on and stop the expansion. The universe will start contracting until all the matter in it collapses to a final singularity, a mirror image of the Big Bang - often dubbed by scientists as the Big Crunch.

This poem uses metaphor to wrestle hopelessly with these themes.

If the universe was an ocean
With gravitational waves,
Planets would be like grains of sand
In underwater caves.

We'd be miniscule like plankton
And there'd be a kind of swish,
As we swim into Andromeda and…
Get gobbled up by fish.

Prisoner of My Dreams

Although I know you're gone for good,
Tonight we're sure to meet.
We'll be together as before -
A jigsaw made complete.

You're a prisoner of my dreams.
At night I find the key.
You're locked away deep in my soul
And I can't set you free.

I hate the clock upon the wall -
Time's stolen you from me,
But when the darkness starts to fall,
My hopes still wander free.

Although you're gone in daylight hours,
And I can't make you stay,
At night I know I'll be with you -
You're just one dream away.

They say there's nothing to fear except fear itself. But, hey, I tell you what, being burned alive bothers me a bit. Also, I'm not too keen on brain-eating parasites.

Low Battery Warning

The battery in my brain's gone dead
I'm clearly not alert -
I checked my watch while drinking tea
And poured it down my shirt.

Should I go to the GP surgery?
My skin has gone all red.
No, I'll see if Halfords has
Some jump leads for my head.

The Sakura Tree

According to ancient Japanese culture, the sakura tree represents the beauty and fragility of life, reminding us that things in life are incredibly precious but also tragically ephemeral.

I remember doors I walked right past,
I remember paths I took too fast;
Nothing's sure or guaranteed.
Hearts may harden, hearts may bleed.

I'm going now, I cannot stay,
Must not look back, just walk away.
If I turn now I know I'll see
Petals fall from a sakura tree.

Tacky Silver Tinsel

The soldier's had no sleep for days,
His face is streaked with sweat.
His shaking fingers fumble
As he lights a cigarette.

Tacky silver tinsel,
Already come undone.
Tacky silver tinsel,
Round the barrel of a gun.

To the sound of dismal wailing,
He staggers from a tent,
Turns red eyes to the soldier,
Breaks off his sad lament.

In the chaos of a war zone,
When everything's unsure,
An empathy between two men
May sometimes still endure.

They hear the sound of gunfire,
But both choose to forget;
Together by the roadside,
They share a cigarette.

Tacky silver tinsel,
Already come undone.
Tacky silver tinsel,
Round the barrel of a gun.

Birth

*Over the course of about 14 billion years, the universe has evolved as a womb of creativity, fusing hydrogen elements into helium to spawn further wombs of creativity, creating galaxies, stars, planets, oceans, mountains, thermophyllic bacteria in deep sea vents, trees, hummingbirds, the music of Chopin and Bach... and you and me. Carbon is the most important energy-transfer molecule in all living cells. We wouldn't exist without it. To produce one single carbon atom, an entire star had to explode! Everything on our planet is the consequence of a 14-billion-year creative process. The stars are **literally** our ancestors.*

According to astronomers,
In whom we have to trust,
A massive star exploded
And formed a cloud of dust.

About five billion years ago,
Or even more perhaps,
The shimmering cloud contracted
And started to collapse.

Just like a womb that brings forth life,
The cloud would soon transform.
As fusion battled gravity,
An infant star was born.

A cloud of simple elements
Around this fiery dome
Accreted dust and soon became
The rock we call our home.

Births like this have taken place
Since time itself began,
From the birth of the universe
Up to the birth of man.

The earth itself is like an egg -
Its inner core's the yolk,
Its mantle is the egg white,
Its shell's the rocky cloak.

The universe is chaotic,
But order is conceived.
Our planet is a living cell,
So wondrous to perceive.

The process goes on everywhere,
In every molecule.
We're connected to the universe…
(We're stardust after all).

Mince Pies

I've got nothing against December,
But time just really flies.
Far too soon we have to face
A year without mince pies!

In the Zone

Sports psychologists describe being "in the zone" as a state of focus that enables athletes in all sports to perform at their peak potential. It involves being totally absorbed in the present (the 'here and now') and processing only those thoughts that help you achieve a particular objective. Many athletes must overcome mental barriers that limit their ability to enter the zone, e.g. self-doubt, fear of failure and over-thinking.

I play a lot of tennis – mainly social doubles – and I've always found it very weird to be "in the zone"!

I don't want to over-think on court,
But I must stay in the zone.
If you attempt a conversation
And it seems like no one's home...
I'm sorry but you'll have to leave
A message after the tone!

Time, the Healer

What if I never get over you
And haunt the past instead,
Or search my heart for echoes
Of all those words unsaid?

If time won't do what it's meant to,
My heart will never mend.
If my thoughts of you persist,
The pain will never end.

My Kingdom for a Horse

I've often thought about joining a local theatre group and getting into acting. But, to be honest, I have enough trouble just being myself.

I don't know where I'm s'posed to sit
If all the world's a stage;
And falling down the trapdoor
Would kill me at my age!

But going to the theatre
Is something I'd endorse.
I'd love to do some Shakespeare -
"My kingdom for a horse!"

You don't need acting talent
Or special repertoire -
They say you should try acting
To find out who you are.

I've heard the local theatre
Is offering a course.
I need to sort out transport...
Now where the hell's that horse?!

The more I try pursuing happiness, the faster it runs away.

Coevolution

If you think about it, a lot of species reciprocally affect each other's evolution, like the eagle and the rabbit...

The weird thing about evolution
Is everyone eventually wins:
While eagles improve their eyesight,
The rabbits run like the wind!

If catching rabbits was easy,
Birds wouldn't need a sharp eye -
They'd slow down and eat at their leisure
And wouldn't bother to fly.

If rabbits evaded the eagles,
Plants would have no defence.
No species gains an advantage…
It's weird, but I guess it makes sense!

Listening for Worms

Earthworms are an excellent source of proteins and minerals for birds all the year round. Blackbirds are endowed with a remarkably acute sense of hearing and can easily detect invertebrates, such as worms, moving under the ground. They can collect as many as two worms every minute in winter!

I was lying on a rug in the garden
And I tried to listen for worms.
My friend was lying there with me,
So we kind of took it in turns.
We abandoned it after an hour or so;
I'm afraid we heard not a squeak.
It's lucky I'm not a blackbird -
I wouldn't survive for a week.

Taken Too Early

Sometimes it's best to talk about
Feelings that rage inside;
Sometimes it's best to hop aboard
And take a cathartic ride.

When life is taken too early,
Like a day that ends at noon,
It flies in the face of all that's right,
Like a year that ends in June.

Nothing can ever prepare you
And nothing can ever be learned,
Grief piles up like heaps of leaves
Just waiting to be burned.

Though the sands ran out too quickly,
My tears will not erase
The memories we made together
That sustain me through these days.

The Role of Air Con Units in the Survival of the Planet

Life on this planet can only exist in a relatively narrow band of temperature. Scientists used to think we benefited from the "right" temperature because the Earth just happened to be the "right" distance from the Sun (93 million miles). But we have since discovered that the sun's temperature has increased by over 25% over the last four billion years. This means that the planet has evidently adapted itself to maintain that vital narrow band of temperature by, for example, drawing more and more carbon dioxide out of the atmosphere. Oh, and air con units maybe?...

The history of life on this planet
Spans four billion years,
But it seems its passage may have been
Stranger than it appears.

If conditions for life were perfect
Four billion years ago,
They were nevertheless different from
The conditions we now know.

Those early days might be considered
Similar, to some extent,
But the heat of the sun has since increased
By twenty five percent.

So either the Earth is adaptable
To changes in our star...
Or air con units are helping us out
More than we think they are!

I Alone Cannot Change the World

I nearly changed the world last night,
As I curled up in my bed.
Solutions to the biggest issues
Sprang up in my head.
Feeling all altruistic,
And, with the curtains drawn,
I resolved to fix world poverty
Before the break of dawn.
As I tried to put the world to rights,
I thought, "No, no, this stinks!
Why should I lie awake all night,
While the world takes forty winks?"

The Time of Day

I confided in my sister
That I really liked her friend.
"She won't give you the time of day,"
My sister did contend.

I wasn't too discouraged,
I knew she'd only mock.
I texted her friend on whatsapp…
She said it's six o'clock.

Hah!!

Always try to keep your feet on the ground if your mind takes a leap in the dark.

Rain Stops Play

England had its fifth wettest autumn on record in 2019, with some areas experiencing a volume of rain unprecedented in modern times. This was bad news for our local tennis club.

There was so much rain in October,
The prospects for tennis were grim,
But people turned up with rod and line
And some even went for a swim!

I was vexed when the chairman implored me
To command the rain to stop…
Do I address it collectively?
Or singly, drop by drop?

Stronger Together

If they warn us a storm is coming,
We'll walk on side by side.
Though barriers lie before us,
We will not be denied.

When darkest clouds are looming,
We will not flinch in fear.
While others dive for cover,
We'll stay together here.

Dark moments may engulf us
And threaten to make us blind -
We'll turn around to face the sun…
The shadows will fall behind.

And when the sun is hidden,
We'll wait for it to rise.
Sometimes what one thinks are weeds
Are flowers in disguise.

Muscle Memory

When I first took up tennis, I was very apprehensive about playing with experienced club players who I perceived to be way better than me (and who I thought were probably sniggering at my inept efforts). But we couldn't afford a coach for my son who was very keen on the sport, so I had to develop my game quickly so that I could hit with him! So, I just practised and practised.

I slowly learned that missing shots is a normal part of playing tennis - the inescapable element of unpredictability. No one ever masters it. That's why you look at the match stats of the top pros and see such a high count of unforced errors. Tiny errors in your footwork or timing or racket angle (or thinking) result in you missing a shot.

So, what you must do is embrace and enjoy the challenge of engaging with all this unpredictability - it's fun trying to master it! Honestly, I love my double faults!! Hmm, okay, not really... but you do have to be a bit philosophical about it and, better still, laugh about it! You can increase the probabilities of doing things right by just playing LOTS more! With all the repetition, you eventually ingrain certain aspects of stroke production into what experts call your 'muscle memory'. You also gradually improve your tactical awareness. And that way, bit by bit, each time you go on court, you raise the level of your capabilities.

It was match day at the tennis club,
I couldn't wait to play;
I thought today my serve would work -
I'd practised every day.

So why on earth did all my serves
Miss by at least a *yard?*
I just don't understand it -
Why is this game so *hard?!*

I'd worked on muscle memory,

Repeating every shot,
But when it came to crunch time,
My muscles just forgot.

Be Afraid... Be Very Afraid!

This Halloween, a friend of mine insisted she was going to brave the freezing cold, the fireworks, the flashing lights and the scary costumes and treat it just like any other night...

It could have been a black cat careering through the streets,
Or maybe trick-or-treaters with flying bags of sweets;
It could have been a hooting owl swooping through the night,
Perhaps a jack-o-lantern's flickering orange light?

What *was* that speedy vortex that startled people so?
Some spooky apparition with nowhere else to go?
Some kind of ghoul or goblin with a wicked sense of fun?...
Just Julie in her hi-vis vest out on her evening run!

Running Late

Buses and trains and boats and planes
Are always running late.
I always turn up right on time
But always have to wait.
The answer shrugs its shoulders,
But still the question begs:
How is it that they run *at all*
When none of them have legs?

The Multiverse

Just as we now accept that the Earth doesn't occupy a special place in the universe, we may soon be obliged to accept that there's nothing particularly special about the observable universe itself. It may just be a small part of a much larger cosmos, containing billions of _un_observable universes, which may or may not boast features similar to the observable one we inhabit.

In theory, a black hole could serve as a tunnel between universes. So, matter and energy falling into the singularity of a black hole could explode out the other side as a 'white hole' in another universe.

Laws that govern our universe
Are now within our reach.
We'll soon have something graspable
To understand and teach.

When scientists get to work out why
Galaxies move apart,
We might find out that actually
We've barely made a start.

Will we ever know it all?
Or is the science perverse?
We could be just a tiny glob
Within a multiverse.

The expanding bubble we call home
May not be all there is -
There may be loads more bubbles
All going pop, bang, fizz!

They say nothing is better than hard work. So, I've decided: nothing is exactly what I'm going to do.

Brand New Hoodie

I saw a hoodie in the store
And thought I'd take a punt.
There was nothing on the label:
The warning should be blunt -
These garments can be harmful
If you wear them back-to-front!

Our Responsibility

We must constantly reorient and retune our understanding of new scientific and demographic knowledge. Faced with numerous existential challenges, we are compelled to develop creative solutions... or surrender to the unintended consequences of past (and current) human activity. Human population levels have increased to the point where we're consuming more resources than the Earth can sustainably provide.

Everything in the universe
Has its own distinctive role.
The stars create the elements,
And atoms make us whole.
Phytoplankton in the oceans
Help us all to breathe.
But now we're here, what should we do?
What should we all bequeath?
Thirteen billion years passed by
Until we came to be,
And now the future's in the hands
Of us...yes, you and me.

Empathic Illness

Have you ever felt someone else's anxiety or physical pain in your own body? Empathic illnesses are those in which you manifest symptoms that are not your own.

I hate it when I know you're ill,
It makes *me* feel bad too.
It might be psychic empathy
Or is it transposed flu?

Well, if it's psychic empathy,
We must work as a team.
Can I suggest a lot of rest
And choccy cake with cream?!

I guess I'll make the best of it,
I'll rest all afternoon…
But I wanna play tennis later -
For god's sake get well soon!

Putting out the Fire

My words won't stop you when you walk out the door,
They don't touch you like they once did before.
I saw the cloud coming but got caught by the rain,
It's no use denying what is perfectly plain.
I could read all the signals, I could see all the signs,
My ears are not deaf and my eyes are not blind.
I'm searching for hope, but hope turns to fear,
I'm scared that my dreams will all disappear.
They tell me time heals, but time's standing still,
They say I'll survive but I don't think I will.
My heart still has faith but my heart is a liar.
It'll take a lot of tears to put out this fire.

Travelling at the speed of light would be so cool, but it wouldn't be without its problems - I suspect people's hats would keep blowing off.

Sun Dance

One of the central religious ceremonies of the Native American Plains Indians was a sun dance, a tribal dance that involved donning special ceremonial attire including buffalo robes, dance bells and feather headdresses.

On the morning of her move to her new flat and on learning that the weather forecast was dire, a friend of mine messaged me requesting that I perform a sun dance. It didn't work...

I'm sorry 'bout my sun dance,
It didn't do the trick;
I twirled around much too fast
And made myself feel sick!

I feel better now, I'll try again,
It'll work this time, I bet!
No, wait, it's raining out there –
My feathers will get wet!

Sometimes

The alleys twisting all around
I was out there lost
But now I've found
That I want you

Sometimes when the sun goes down
I think I feel you
All around
And I want you

But of course you're never there
And all is empty
All is bare
And I want you

The Great Clownfish Discovery

We may be simple clownfish,
But don't take us for fools.
I'm sure you will have learned by now
That most fish swim in schools.

As an educated species,
It was our firm belief
That the universe did not extend
Beyond the coral reef.

Imagine my surprise that day
(A day I won't forget),
When I was hoisted from the sea
In a scuba diver's net!

A new world was revealed to me,
Of water quite bereft,
I saw a boat, a strange blue sky,
Weird creatures right and left.

Anyway, I thought I'd better
Confess to you my crime -
I hijacked your quite foolish book
To tell you this in rhyme!

Here's my new (very) short story. It's in the suspense genre. Will they publish it?....................No. The end.

Counting Sheep

I'm lying in bed, trying to snooze,
Just watching the sheep filing past.
If I were to count them all in twos,
Would I fall asleep twice as fast?

Earth

Recent studies suggest that there are several hundred quintillion planets in the universe, but only one like Earth. Scientists insist it's special. They say our sun is just the right age to produce the heavier chemical elements required for life. Allegedly, we're protected from catastrophic collisions with asteroids and comets by the proximity of Jupiter and its vast gravitational pull. Cosmologists insist the Earth was also lucky to have stumbled into a planet-like object called Theia a few billion years ago. Having swallowed Theia's iron core, our planet acquired the strong geomagnetic field that deflects harmful particles streaming from the Sun. And, of course, you'll have heard all the stuff about our fortuitous "Goldilocks" position in the "habitable zone" of the solar system, where we're free from sterilising radiation emanating from black holes and supernovae and we have the right conditions for liquid water, etc, etc.

Yeah, but, I don't know… was it <u>really</u> so difficult to create this planet?

You take a planet and call it Earth
And spin it round for all its worth,
And once the sun is close enough,
You fill it up with people and stuff.

SIMPLE!

Some birds can navigate by the stars...

Memories

Nobody walks beside me
And days switch off and on;
The marble dreams are molten now,
Just fragments weeping on.

The corn field humped in silence,
Cringing in its pain.
We once walked here together,
Singing in the rain.

In memories of monochrome,
I hear a sad refrain.
I hope the colours will return,
I hope we'll sing again.

Cyberspace Germs

Your emails are contagious!
I read one you just wrote -
You said you had a nasty cold
And a sore and swollen throat.

Before I read one sentence,
I felt compelled to sneeze,
And hours after I finished it,
The symptoms hadn't eased.

I wheezed and coughed for ages,
My throat was really red.
I grabbed a box of tissues
And went upstairs to bed.

I think I'll go to PC World
And find that salesman bloke.
I installed their antivirus -
That software is a joke!

The Catskill Eagle

This poem is dedicated to my daughter. It pays homage to a quote by one of my favourite writers, Herman Melville…

Oh, behold the Catskill eagle,
So majestic and so high.
It spies a deep, dark gorge below
And dives out of the sky.

But even in its lowest swoop,
The air that it patrols
Is high up in the mountains…
Just like some people's souls!

Reading Past My Bedtime

I take my kindle to bed each night
And no matter how exciting the prose,
It always sends me straight to sleep
And the kindle lands on my nose!

Where *Is* Everybody?

The Fermi paradox, named after Italian-American physicist Enrico Fermi, seeks to answer the question as to why we seem to be alone in space. It expresses the apparent contradiction between the lack of evidence for extraterrestrial civilisations and the high estimates for the probability of their existence. Some astrophysicists have used the Drake equation, a formula that seeks to quantify the odds of intelligent alien life, to indicate the likelihood of interstellar travel and communication by spacefaring races… and they've concluded that our planet should certainly have been visited by aliens by now.

A civilised race with rockets and stuff
And a bit of ambition and drive
Could surely colonise the Milky Way,
So why do they never arrive?
Perhaps they all tend to self-destruct
Or assume we'll react out of fear.
The odds of intelligent alien life
Suggest they should now be here!

Where *is* everybody???

Sometimes I think we're all alone,
Sometimes I think we're not.
Either way, I have to say,
It boggles my mind a lot!

Lunch Matters

The days seem to go so quickly now
And it may be no more than a hunch,
But I'm freaked by the possibility
That I might have missed yesterday's lunch!

When faced with serious questions like those raised in this book, I think it's okay to give up and go fishing.

The Anthropocene

Scientists contend that human-driven biological, chemical and physical changes to the Earth have now become so significant that they herald an entirely new epoch – the Anthropocene. It's not good enough to passively accept that the destiny of the universe is determined by self-organising dynamics and that humanity is powerless to influence this. Humanity is an integral part of those dynamics. We need to be agents of change.

In the unfolding tale of the cosmos,
Humanity is now on the page,
And the challenge that lies before us
Must be one with which we'll engage.

For we're part of a living universe,
And what might all of this mean?
Empathy and knowledge and wonder -
We're in the Anthropocene.

Religious communities in this world
Should no longer dwell apart
From those on the secular side of things
If we want to make a good start.

Rational and aesthetic fulfilment
May be ours if we can define
A narrative to guard and guide us
While humans and nature entwine.

I Met My Wife in Venice

People often ask me where I met my wife, who is Italian. We didn't meet anywhere in particular – we just grew up in the same neighbourhood. But sometimes it's fun to embellish the story a little, so I say we met in Venice (well, hey, her family come from that area).

I met my wife in Venice.
I said, "Why are you *here*?
You told me you were just popping out
For crisps and cans of beer!"

Tennis Serving Tips

I served a lot of double faults,
Frustration grew and grew,
But then I found a strategy
I'd like to share with you.

So, when I serve in tennis,
I try to use disguise -
I step up to the baseline
With a mask over my eyes.

Variety is the next best thing,
So let it be your guide -
Put your hat on backwards
And sometimes to the side.

And if these tips don't work for you,
You might try one more thing:
If all else fails, just stay at home
And be the Xbox king!

Earthrise

From the moment NASA astronaut, Bill Anders, took his iconic photo of the Earthrise from the far side of the moon in 1968, we started to envision a new context for our planet. It inspired awe and wonder. Whether or not it galvanised the environmental movement, as has been claimed, it certainly marked the moment when a collective global consciousness truly arrived.

If you transcend reality
Like religious people do,
The world will bite you really hard.
I guess I'll pray for you.

If you exploit the planet Earth
By burning coal and stuff,
The world will buckle and become
A nightmare soon enough.

Where can we find a role for us?
Can answers be foreseen
In science or humanities...
Or in the space between?

If it seems so unimportant
To work out why we're here,
NASA's photo of the Earthrise
May help to make it clear.

Thank You Letter

That embarrassing moment when you can't remember who gave you what...

Thank you so much, dear Auntie of mine.
You seem to read my mind!
You choose the right present ev'ry time -
So thoughtful and so kind.

If people misuse it, I'll give 'em short shrift;
I'll keep it in the closet.
I'm incredibly grateful for the gift...
Oh, by the way, what *was* it?

Oh no, this is really unpleasant!
I can't send this now, because,
Although I've remembered the present,
I don't know which auntie it was!

Writing on the Wall

Does "liking" someone's status
Mean anything at all?
Am I really getting close to you
By writing on your wall?

I guess we all have busy lives
And have no time to spend,
So we simply click a button
To call someone a "friend".

It could be social networking
Is not what we assume,
And loneliness is the elephant
That's unseen in the room.

We don't like getting too intense
And won't pick up the phone;
To me it doesn't make much sense…
We're all in this alone.

Missing Emails

When my friend moved from Reading to Goring (about 10 miles away), for some reason emails inexplicably went missing...

Now you've moved so far away,
Our emails need more time -
Now there's all those fields to cross,
And all those hills to climb.

Perhaps we should both bear in mind:
Each email that we send
Could be drinking in the Pack Horse pub
Or dozing at Cane End!

Please Miss, There's a Problem With the Baby Jesus!

In my last year at Alfred Sutton Primary School, we performed a traditional nativity play in front of parents and teachers. I was very proud to have been given a speaking part. I wasn't Joseph or one of the Wise Men or even the Angel Gabriel, but First Shepherd seemed challenging enough at the time. Accompanied by two other shepherds and a couple of loudly baa-ing sheep, I took to the stage with a towel on my head and someone's grandad's walking stick for a crook...

In my one and only acting role,
Way back in primary school,
I was cast as leading shepherd.
I felt like such a fool...

I pointed to the tinsel star,
But no one heard me speak -
I was muffled by my woollen beard
And drowned out by the sheep!

Things got worse as the night wore on. The lowest point was probably when Helen, playing the part of Mary, managed to drop Baby Jesus and his head fell off. One of the donkeys picked it up and handed it back to her.

Question Marks

I don't understand what caused the pain,
It was one that both of us shared.
We tried to shield one another,
But neither of us was spared.

Above the pain were question marks,
Ones we couldn't erase,
Questions without any answers
That hung there for days and days.

With the passage of time, I'm glad to say
I no longer feel the pain,
But I don't think we have a solution -
The question marks remain.

Tribalism

A lot of people define themselves
By the football club they support.
They often resort to tribalism
And don't behave like they ought.

Sadly, the same kind of tribalism
Is now rife in society.
I wish politicians would lead the way
With grace and propriety.

Good Ol' Gravity

When Edwin Hubble trained his telescope at the night sky during the 1920s, he was the first cosmologist to determine that the Milky Way is not the only galaxy in the universe. Not only do we now know there are billions of galaxies, but we have also determined that they're all rushing away from each other.

Once, the observable universe
Was the size of a grain of sand.
Now it's a trillion galaxies
And continues to expand.

As it zooms with acceleration,
It fills my mind with awe.
I'm so grateful that good ol' gravity
Keeps my feet on the floor.

Lockdown Blues

The covid-19 pandemic and the subsequent restrictive measures gave rise to a whole new raft of challenges (and a whole new vocabulary) in 2020. People turned into 'coughin' dodgers', recoiling in terror at the sound of someone innocuously clearing their throat. We had to cope with cabin fever. And I'm sure many of us experienced an emotional coronacoaster as we enjoyed the calm and peacefulness one minute and then wept with anxiety the next.

I've been buying only essentials
And obeying the government rules.
I've been doing the clapping for carers
And plenty of video calls.

I've run out of pasta and loo rolls
And queued at the chemist for meds.
I've done quizzes with friends on Zoom
And seen just the tops of their heads!

I've been planning more running and walking,
But I haven't persuaded my legs.
In the stores, I've kept to two metres,
And danced in the aisles when there's eggs!

I've promised to write a to-do-list,
But each day I go and forget.
I've bought lots of books for my kindle,
But haven't got round to them yet.

I've remembered that Mondays are bin days
And made sure they're out there by eight;
And then I've discovered it's Tuesday –
I'm twenty-four hours too late!

I've watched all the daily news briefings
And marvelled at all of the stats;
When R equals one, I nod wisely
And pretend I've grasped all the facts.

I've bought wine for that special occasion,
When the end of the lockdown's in sight...
But then I've succumbed to temptation
And drunk it the very same night!

Is there light at the end of the tunnel?
Or is it an oncoming train?
I hope you cope better than I do...
I can't wait to see you again.

The Huddle

We have a lot of soft toys around the house. For some reason, a large majority of them are penguins. During the coronavirus pandemic, I had a dream that they all became fed up with the UK's social distancing measures and decided to leave.

I couldn't find my penguins.
Where might they all have gone?
Did they waddle to the local pub
While there's a lockdown on?

Did I find them in the lounge bar,
All huddled round for lunch?
Icebergers on the menu -
Peck, nibble, nibble, crunch!

Did they come back home again
And dance around in pairs?
Were some of them so tipsy,
They fell back down the stairs?

Nothing is impossible,
But if you think it through:
Penguins can't climb up the stairs -
So, no, it can't be true!...

Fact is, they got arrested,
(I learned by word of mouth),
For huddling far too closely...
And now they've flown down south!

The End

If there's a parallel universe,
This book may well appear
With opulent words and imagery…
But *you're* stuck with *this* I fear!

No symbolism or lyricism,
And jokes that make you groan -
Its only 'ism' is multiversism
With qualities all its own!

So, I hope you enjoyed the journey?
I shouldn't think you did.
But it cost you just an hour or so…
And maybe three or four quid?

Anyway, thanks for sticking with it -
You've seen me at my worst!
And as you've suffered quite enough…
That's it! There's no more verse!!!

INDEX

A Trip to Mars 6

Be Afraid… Be Very Afraid! 69

Birds on a Telegraph Wire 12

Birth 51

Brand New Hoodie 73

Checkmate 39

Coevolution 58

Counting Sheep 82

Cozzzmology 29

Cyberspace Germs 86

Dark Matter 16

Dominique 36

Earth 83

Earthrise 95

Empathic Illness 75

Forsaking the Poppy 22

Friends 15

Good Ol' Gravity 103

I Alone Cannot Change the World 62

I Met My Wife in Venice.. 93

Ikea 7

In the Zone 54

Insert Name Here 18

I've Changed My Mind 24

Laryngitis 17

Listening for Worms 59

Lockdown Blues... 104

Low Battery Warning 47

Lunch Breaks.. 42

Lunch Matters 90

Make It Snow This Christmas... 30

Memories.. 85

Mince Pies 53

Missing Emails... 99

Muscle Memory 67

My Kingdom for a Horse.. 56

No Protons, No Electrons and Just a Dash of Milk 2

Our Responsibility... 74

Over the Edge 43

'Owellojello' Gemma 32

Paradoxically Pooped 27

Pieces of Truth 38

Please Miss, There's a Problem With the Baby Jesus! 100

Prisoner of My Dreams 45

Putting out the Fire 76

Question Marks 101

Rain Stops Play 65

Random 41

Reading Past My Bedtime 88

Running Late 70

Silenced by the Bullet 34

Six Degrees of Separation 25

Six Minutes 11

Sometimes 79

Sorry! 5

Stronger Together 66

Sun Dance 78

Tacky Silver Tinsel 49

Taken Too Early 60

Tartan Trainers 28

Tennis Serving Tips 94

Thank You Letter 96

The Anthropocene 92

The Catskill Eagle 87

The End 107

The End of the Universe or the Big Munch 44

The Faithful Moth 21

The Great Clownfish Discovery 80

The Huddle.. 106

The Multiverse.. 71

The Role of Air Con Units in the Survival of the Planet.................. 61

The Sakura Tree.. 48

The Teapot 13

The Time of Day 63

The Universe in a Tennis Ball 19

Those Two Impostors.. 3

Time, the Healer 55

Tribalism 102

Two Wolves... 1

When the Bubble Bursts 9

Where *Is* Everybody?... 89

Writing on the Wall.. 98

120

ABOUT THE AUTHOR

David Winship has written an unauthorised autobiography and several critically disdained literary tomes. His work is frequently compared with Steinbeck, Orwell and Hemingway, but unfortunately Mike Steinbeck, Daisy Orwell and Howard Hemingway were all terrible writers. He has been totally overlooked for the most prestigious literary awards worldwide, which is a shame as most of the words are spelled correctly. In fact, his books contain material that ranks with the finest literary works in history: all the right letters are there, just not necessarily in the right order.

Other books by David Winship

Could Have Been Verse, 2018, ISBN 978-1981012350

The Moon Pigeon, 2019, ISBN 978-1090321937

The Battle of Trafalgar Square, 2018, ISBN 978-1724086884

ANTimatter, 2018, ISBN 978-1986340724

ANTidote, 2016, ISBN 978-1530860722

Through the Wormhole, Literally, 2015, ISBN 978-1508718406

Stirring the Grass, 2016, ISBN 978-1492952725

Off the Frame, 2001, ISBN 978-1482793833

Talking Trousers and Other Stories, 2013, ISBN 978-1484898420

Printed in Great Britain
by Amazon

85418682R00078